Lark

Amy Richie

Published by Amy Richie, 2017.

LARK

First edition. December 30, 2017.

Copyright © 2017 Amy Richie.

ISBN: 979-8223031550

Written by Amy Richie.

For Renae

Be your own kind of bird and stretch those wings.

Chapter One

"Have you ever wondered what it would be like to fly?" Her face tilted upwards until it caught the light from the almost full moon.

"Like in an airplane?" I pulled my jacket tighter to my chest, pausing slightly to take in how fast my heart was hammering along.

Angela had always been just a little different than other girls; maybe that was why I liked her so much. Or maybe it was the way she pushed her full lips out to a frown when I hesitated to come out and meet her.

I was no goody two shoes, but 1:30 in the morning was pushing it – even for Angela.

"Not in an airplane," she grinned, shaking her head hard enough to make the pony tail she had piled high on top of her head bounce. "Just to fly free."

"I..." I sucked in a breath, already trying to find an excuse to go back inside. "No, I haven't," I finished lamely.

"We're not even old enough to drive a car yet," she sighed.

I watched as her lips pushed out from her mouth again, wondering suddenly what it would feel like to kiss a girl like Angela Lake.

"Not much longer though," I offered with an awkward smile. Hopefully she wouldn't be able to tell where my thoughts had strayed to. "A few more months."

"Maybe for you, Jacob," her full bottom lip disappeared inside her closed mouth, "not for me."

Besides my nan on dad's side, who only saw me twice a year – Angela was the only one who called me Jacob. No matter how many times I told her not to.

"Well," I swallowed back my words, unsure if I should be making a promise I wasn't sure I could keep. She looked at me, her dark blue eyes that I swear turned purple the longer I looked at her, were opened as wide as her eyelids would allow.

"Well what?" She prompted.

"When I get my license," I lurched ahead anyways, "I'll give you a ride. My mom says she'll buy me a truck when I turn sixteen."

"It'll be too late by then," she half smiled.

"Too late for what?" Like 1:30 in the morning wasn't late.

"Well," she wiggled her eyebrows playfully, "who knows, by then maybe I'll have flown away already."

I stood there awkwardly, not sure what kind of response she was waiting for as she stared at me. "You can just wait to fly," I shrugged.

"When I was little," she crouched low to the ground, bending even lower down to the sidewalk, "I wanted to be a mermaid so I could swim with the sharks."

"Sharks?" Why couldn't she try normal on for once and say dolphins?

"They wouldn't eat mermaids," she giggled.

Oh yeah, I almost forgot she was pretending to be a mermaid. "I've never wanted to be a mermaid." I glanced back at my dark house and up at the window on the second floor that was mine. Why had I woken up to the tiny plunks of pebbles hitting the glass? And what possessed me to sneak out and meet the girl who had thrown them?

"What do you think would be better – to be a mermaid or a unicorn?" She grinned up at me.

Angela could have been attractive, I realized with a jolt to my stomach, maybe even pretty, if only she would brush her hair once in a while. And what was wrong with a girl putting on a little make up?

"Are those my only options?" I mumbled through the lump that had somehow formed in my throat.

"You could be a ninja, I suppose, but they don't really do anything special."

"What are you talking about? Ninja's are special. They got mad fighting skills."

"Yes. But can they fly?"

"If we were meant to fly, we'd have wings."

She laughed loudly, the sound bursting from the lips that were now hidden from me as she bent over the ground. "That sounds like something my mother would say."

"I thought your mom was dead."

I don't know what made me say it. Maybe it was the lateness of the night or maybe it was because I was distracted by what I could just see was something she was drawing. As soon as the words were out, I regretted them. I knew it wasn't something we should talk about.

I glanced over at the house right next to my own, equally dark, the one that belonged to Angela and her father. I could still remember the day they had moved here from the city. We were only eight and just barely understood words like 'mugging' and 'murder.' Who knew things like that really existed in the world?

"I'm...sorry," I back peddled.

"It's ok." She stood up and brushed her white fingers on the thighs of her dark jeans. "You're right, she is dead."

To avoid looking directly at her and her strangely purple eyes, I studied the drawing she had just created. At least a hundred small lines joined together to form the intricate shape of a butterfly with four letters written in the wings. "AL and JW." Written separately, but still connected.

"Is that supposed to be us?"I blurted a little too loudly.

"It's supposed to be a butterfly." She dipped down to add a few more lines.

"I mean the letters. Angela Lake and Jake Winoton?" My forehead creased as I studied the chalk drawing.

She shrugged her thin shoulders. "We're friends, aren't we?"

No, we're not – I wanted to tell her. I can't be your friend Angela, otherwise people won't talk to me either .i don't want anyone to think we're friends.

Instead, I felt my head nodding it's own agreement. "I guess so."

Her lips puckered up and then flattened ot as her smile grew, unexpectantly making my breath catch. I wasn't really going to be her friend, I told myself. But I couldn't just say that to her face.

"Then by way of apology," she announced, "I'll accept your offer."

"What offer?"

"To take me for a ride."

"When I get my license?" My ears grew hot despite the chill in the air.

"Nope," she shook her head back and forth, "right now. Tonight."

Chapter Two

"Tonight?" I felt the lines in my forehead grow deeper. "We can't go for a ride tonight. I'm not even supposed to be out of my house; my mom would never..."

"We're not going to ask your mom," she widened her eyes briefly. "Your brother has a truck, we can use his."

"No way." I almost laughed at her, sure that she was only kidding, except those lips of hers pouted back out. "That's crazy."

"No one will ever even know," she insisted, her eyes staying wide.

"I don't know how to drive." I blow my breath out through my nose, irritated all over again at the girl most people avoided.

"You already told me last summer that your dad taught you to drive." She finally lowered her eyes, allowing me to breath freely again.

"Not so I could steal Jimmy's truck and drive my neighbor girl around in it."

Angela shrugged. "You don't know why he taught you. He's dead now."

I couldn't get mad at her for throwing my own words back at me. I could only turn my head, running the toe of my shoe over her chalk lines. "Yeah, he is."

"It's ok to be afraid, Jacob." She spoke gently, sounding older than any of the girls we went to school with. "But you're the only one I could come to. The only one who would take me for a drive."

It took too long for me to respond. She knew even before I did that I would give in and do as she asked. I saw the side of her face light up with her grin and realized it myself.

"We can't go far," I sighed.

"Not far." She held up one hand.

"And it's only if I can get the keys."

I already knew where the spare keys hung just above the kitchen door. Keys that had always been and should have always been perfectly safe to hang there. It would barely take a full minute to run inside and grab them. No one would ever know, just like Angela said.

"Wait by the truck," I ordered gruffly, excitement and nerves fighting for precedence inside of me.

How in the world had I gotten myself into a situation that had me tiptoeing through our dark living room? I should have been sleeping in my warm bed upstairs. My hands hesitated, hoovering just over the single key that glared at me.

How long would she wait if I just didn't go back outside? So what if she got mad – it wasn't like we were friends. Or I could go back out there and tell her I couldn't get the key.

I could have done either of those things, but instead I snatched the cool metal between my fingers and darted back out to the night where Angela waited for me. I smiled back at her despite myself, excitement finally winning out over the nerves.

As a general rule, I kept my rule breaking to a minimum. Keeping the internet on until way after eleven; watching the latest episode of my favorite TV show before my homework was really done, and even the occasional swear word when mom couldn't hear me. This was big.

"Did you get it?" She squealed, jumping up and down a fe times when I flashed the silver key at her.

"I can't believe we're doing this," I laughed, shaking my head.

"It's a great adventure," she threw her arms open wide, "the ninja and the mermaid."

But who ever heard of a ninja and a mermaid going anywhere together – adventure or not? They wouldn't be able to live in each other's worlds. Tonight wasn't a night for rules, though.

"Come on little mermaid," I teased, "your carriage awaits."

Angela clapped her hands together and did her stupid little dance again. "Too bad I don't have red hair."

"It's kind of red."

"It is not," she whined, leading the way to the big black truck parked in our garage.

Being from a small town, the doors of the truck were unlocked and the garage door was left hanging open until the snow started flying. Luck was on our side – or maybe it was something stronger than luck.

"I like your hair though," I complimented off handedly. Situating myself on the seat next to her with the steering wheel in my lap brought on a fresh wave of nerves.

"You do?" Her bottom lip disappeared inside her mouth again.

"Yeah. I mean," I shrugged lightly, "it'd probably look nicer if you brushed it more than once a month, but it's still nice."

"I brush it more than once a month!" Her laughter exploded, filling up the cab of the truck and seeping all the way into me.

Angela wasn't so bad, not really.

"Okay, okay," I held my hand up in the small space between us, "maybe twice."

"Jacob!" She swatted my arm in mock anger. "Easy for you to say something like that, you don't have to brush your hair at all."

"Yes I do," I crinkled my nose in her direction.

There was something about her that I couldn't quite define. Always, I tried my best to ignore the feeling of lightness and freedom she gave me just by being beside her; instead trying to focus on the names the other girls called her. It never failed though – five minutes in her presence, and every guard I worked so hard to put up crumbled away, I don't know what it was about her.

"Ready?" I asked, sucking in a sharp breath.

"Yep." She nodded enthusiastically and sat up straighter in her seat.

"I'm a little nervous," I admitted in a rush of jittery laughter.

"I'm not," she turned to me, blue eyes wide, "I trust you completely."

Why did she have to go and say something like that? Like I wasn't nervous enough already without her going all weird on me again.

"Glad one of us does," I mumbled, carefully shoving the key into the ignition.

Chapter Three

"Where should we go?" I asked softly, nerves making my throat thicker than normal.

Backing out of the driveway had been easier than I anticipated. It had been almost a year since my dad had taught me to drive, just as long since I'd been behind a wheel. I expected it to be harder to remember all the details, but it was easy.

My heart stuttered and dropped down to my stomach when a car passed us. The only people out this late had to be a police officer. If I got pulled over, my mom would kill me. Then my brother would kill me so I'd be dead twice.

We didn't get pulled over though, whether it was a cop or not, and now we were driving slowly through a sleeping town. There had been no talk of a destination; in fact, as far as planning went – we had nothing. We just went.

"We could go to the orchid," she suggested just as softly.

Was she nervous too? I chanced a quick peak her way, but her profile gave nothing away. Same pouty lips and eyes wide open.

"The orchid?"

"Yeah." Her head bobbed in my peripheral vision.

The orchid had once been a vibrant place that grew red apples so big it took two hands to hold them. All that was just hear say though, since the place had been neglected for more years than Angela and I had been alive. It was just a few dozen trees overgrown and shapeless now.

The orchid was mostly used by couples who had no other place to make out. Why would she want to go there?

Like my night had been going so far, I agreed despite my better judgement.

1:30 on a Tuesday night, it wasn't surprising that we didn't run into any other cars on our seven mile drive to the orchid. I pulled the truck deep into the trees and killed the engine.

The silence was shockingly loud.

"You're a good driver," Angela was the first to cut into the silence, her voice soft and gentle.

"Yeah?" I felt my lips tighten with my grin. My dad had always said I was a natural, it was nice to hear it again – even if it wasn't from him.

"We didn't get in a wreck or anything."

That was true, I conceded with relief, we had gotten here ok. I still wasn't sure why we were here or why it was so important that we go tonight, but it felt good that I was able to do it.

"It's kinda creepy out there, huh?" I jerked my chin towards the windshield where the misshapen trees were clearly visible.

"No," her voice came out slightly breathy, "it's not creepy."

I looked again, just to be sure the trees hadn't been chopped down and replaced by something less grotesque. Like statues; although a few dozen stone statues all clumped together for no apparent reason might be worse than overgrown apple trees.

But no, they were still there, their branchy arms paused midway in an ancient dance they had been forced to stop. Nope, nothing creepy about that at all. "What would you call it then?" I scowled.

"Sad."

At least she didn't say something stupid like beautiful or amazing. It was awkward when she started acting too weird.

"Do you want to get out now?"

My head jerked back slightly at the suggestion. Were we going to get out? Was it even safe to walk around here at night?

"Shouldn't we stay in here?"

"Why?"

Of course she would ask me something like that. "I don't know," I shrugged, "just thought we should."

"I want to see the stars."

"You can see them out the window," I offered, tilting my forehead into the glass in an effort to see the sky. Maybe not.

"it's not the same." Her tongue clicked against the roof of her mouth at almost the same time her door clicked open.

Should I follow her? I didn't have to. She had asked for a ride in the truck, not a creepy walk through an overgrown orchid. Who knew what kind of animals lived out there? I could just stay right where I was and wait for her to be finished looking at the stars.

Her pale form disappeared around the end of the truck. "Ugh!" I groaned loudly, flipping my own handle up.

I'd just go make her get back in the truck ,I told myself as I made my own way to the end of the truck. We weren't going to be staying out here.

Angela stood with her back against the tailgate and her arms folded over her chest. The tendons in her neck stretched tight as she leaned her head back to see the sky.

I ran my tongue quickly across my bottom lip, wondering for the hundredth time what I had been thinking to come outside tonight and meet Angela Lake. Pressing my finger against my mouth, I joined her next to the tailgate. A few minutes wouldn't hurt anything.

"I can't believe there are so many stars up there," her voice filled with wonder, making her sound like a little kid.

Hadn't she ever seen the night sky before? "There's a bunch," I agreed, glancing briefly upwards, we probably could have seen them just as well from our own houses.

Chapter Four

"Do you know what that one is called?" She raised her arm as far as it would go and pointed upwards.

How was I supposed to know what the name of some star was? There were too many for all of them to have names. "Nope," My lips popped on the word.

My head rested next to Angela's in the bed of the truck, both of us sprawled out on our backs. It was the closest I'd been to her since we were kids. Weird – but a good weird.

"My dad knows the names of the stars," she declared matter-of-factly.

"All of them?"

"Yeah."

I doubted that was true. We all used to believe our dad's were superman and knew everything. Then one day, they just weren't, and we finally could see them for what they really were. Just grown up versions of us; still confused and half scared most of the time. They didn't know everything and it turns out they aren't invincible either.

"Not all of them even have names," I scoffed. I was being mean to her, and I wasn't even sure why.

"Shows how much you know."

I heard the smugness in her voice and for some reason that made me even more mad. Having lived next door to her all this time, this wasn't the first time I was confronted by her strange way of looking at things.

"Maybe," I shrugged, giving up quickly on the argument. "Are you ready to get back now?"

"We just got here," she pouted. "We can stay for a little longer."

I glanced around us nervously. So far we had been lucky – no one had caught us leaving and we got here ok. Still, it didn't feel right to keep pushing our luck.

It didn't seem likely, but I really hoped that no one would ever find out that I had come out here in the middle of the night wit hAngela Lake. I would never be able to live something like that down.

"Were you sad when your dad died?"

My heart stuttered slightly at her question. What kind of thing was that to ask someone? Wan't it obvious?

"Yeah." My throat felt a little tight so I pressed my lips together.

"Did he know he would die?" She asked, moving her full lips into a frown.

"I don't know," I scowled, uncomfortable with the way the conversation was going, "it's not like we talked about it."

"Not at all?" She pressed on.

"No," I shrugged. "Why would we?"

"I don't know," she shrugged too, "but it seems like something that might come up."

"Most people don't talk about dying." Just because her and her dad were weirdos didn't mean we all were.

"It's a natural thing though – like...farting or sneezing."

"You're so weird," I blurted out, laughing a little at myself for saying it out loud and at her for saying something that warranted it.

"I've heard that one before," she giggled.

"From me?" One eyebrow cocked high on my forehead. I couldn't remember ever calling her weird to her face before – no matter how man times I had thought it.

"Yeah, from you," she chuckled. "Remember the time I ate that grasshopper?"

"Oh yeah," I smiled wide. It had been almost a year ago now, but I did remember the day Angela had grossed us all out by eating a live grasshopper – all because she'd seen it on TV.

"It didn't taste too bad," she shrugged.

"And you wonder why I called you weird," I shook my head, my smile growing wider. "You would never catch me eating a bug – no matter why."

"That's because you're not brave." She raised her chin in my direction.

"Maybe not," I conceded. Out in the orchid the wind had started to pick up, forcing the ghostly branches into a lively dance. Hopefully it wouldn't start storming before we made it back home.

"I remember when my mom died," she said softly.

I stiffened slightly. We weren't supposed to talk about her mother – not ever. But mom had only said not to mention her, she hadn't said what to do if Angela brought her up.

"You were young," I muttered out.

"I still remember."

"I never said you didn't."

"My dad cried."

"That was his wife," I pointed out. Of course he would cry.

"It was the first time I'd ever seen him cry."

Not knowing what else to say, I only nodded.

"I was more scared of him crying than I was of anything else."

"He was just being human – he probably couldn't help it."

"He told me that sometimes we hurt so much that our hearts cry and then it leaks out of our eyes."

Of course he did.

"Did your mom cry when your dad died?'

"Yeah," I mumbled, uncomfortable all over again.

And I knew exactly what Angela meant when she said that was the scariest part. I wouldn't easily forget the day I had found my mom crumpled up on the side of her bed. The funeral was already over and empty dishes had been returned to helpful family and friends.

For a heart stopping minute, I had thought she died too, but then her shoulders started to shake and I heard the sobs that seemed to tear out of her throat like a wild animal. I stood there in her doorway, my heart hammering away like a mad man, until finally I couldn't take any more. I turned away and practically ran back to my own bedroom.

I didn't cry, I just sat there staring at nothing. I don't know how long I sat there before mom stuck her head in the door to ask if I was hungry. Without a word, I followed her downstairs to watch her make grilled cheese sandwiches.

"Of course she cried," I told Angela. "Why wouldn't she?"

Chapter Five

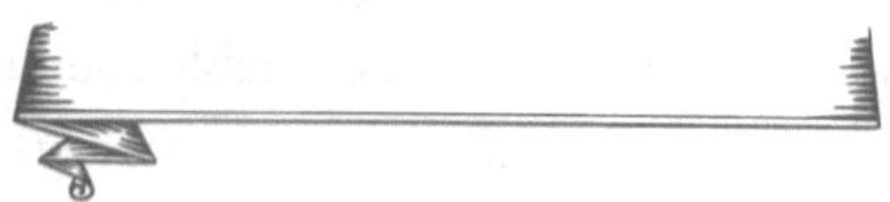

"Let's walk," Angela suddenly suggested.

"Walk where?" I narrowed my eyes, wary of this new idea. So far following her plans had ended up with us miles from home in the middle of the night with a stolen truck.

"Through the trees." She swung her arm out wide as if it were obvious.

"I don't think that's a good idea."

"Why not?" She smiled wide and scooted all the way to the edge of the truck. "I think it's a great idea." With that she flung herself down to the ground.

"Angela," I hissed into the darkness. "Get back here." There was no answer. "Where are you?"

"Come on Jacob," she called out gently. "Be brave."

Be brave? Would running after my insane neighbor through a creepy orchid in the middle of the night really make me brave? Or would it just make me as crazy as her?

I chewed nervously on the inside of my lip. Any way I looked at it, I couldn't just let her go running off by herself. What if she got hurt? What if it was bad enough that I had to take her to the hospital? Then we'd be caught for sure.

With a short sigh, I jumped down from the back of the truck.

"Alright," I called out, "I'm coming so wait up." Of course she didn't answer. Had I ever expected her to? "Angela!"

A ghostly sounding laugh came back to me, coming from the shadows of the tree just in front of me. Were we really going to play hide and seek out here?

"Angela," I yelled, scanning the black spots for her, "come on, stop messing around."

There was a flash of color and a flutter of material as she came into view for a second, then disappeared again. My pulse jumped unexpectantly. I wasn't really going to chase after her – was I?

Almost against my will, my feet shuffled forward, towards the place Angela had just been. "Hey," I called out again, my tongue flickered over my bottom lip. "Angela?" Taking a deep breath I lunged forward around the same tree I had seen her standing behind. She was gone.

"Jacob!" She called out, laughing softly, "You'll have to be faster than that if you want to catch me."

I looked up in time to see her wide smile before she turned and ran full out. Not even trying to hold back my own laughter, I tore off after her.

"You really think you can outrun me?" I taunted, gathering speed as I saw the pattern the trees made. Even though they were grown over, it was easy to see where the old ones were, "I'm gonna get you Angela, there's no where to hide."

She gave a tiny scream when I rounded the tree she was crouched behind and reached my arms out to grab her. My fingers just skimmed off her waist before she twirled out of reach again.

"You can't catch me, Jacob," she squealed, taking off again.

Angela didn't bother to stay in the safety of the overgrown rows, instead darting behind trees and cutting clear across. That was just like her though – never staying in the lines.

Not wanting to lose her completely, I cut across two rows and continued my sprint. Hopefully no sneaky tree roots would try and trip me up. That was all I needed – a broken ankle.

I could just make out the back of her shirt as she ducked behind another tree. Did she really think she would be able to hide there? It wasn't like the trees were very thick. Crouching low to the ground, I made my way over to where she hid.

"Gotcha," I screeched, making a mad grab into thin air. Angela wasn't there.

My confusion made my eyebrows pucker up and meet in the middle. She had been here, I saw her. No way could she get away without me noticing. Where was she then?

I Whirled around on the spot, suddenly sure she was standing right behind me. She wasn't. I began walking down the same path I had seen her on before, moving slower so I could check behind all the trees.

I could just imagine her crouching low in her hiding place with her hand pressed over her mouth to stop from laughing out loud and giving away her position. I grinned wide at the sight my mind made up.

"Angela," I sing-songed her name in a low voice. "I'm coming for you."

Up ahead, still several feet away, grew a tree that was at least twice the width of any of the others around it. The perfect hiding place.

Harnessing my inner lion, I crouched low to the ground again and made a wide arc so I could approach the tree from the other side. She wouldn't be able to get away this time.

I figured she would probably be able to hear me once I got too close, so I through caution to the wind and made a dash the rest of the way. Angela wasn't there either, though.

"What?" My eyebrows shot low on my forehead. Where was she?

This was Angela Lake we were talking about though, the weirdest girl in school. She wouldn't get all cute and claim fear of the trees and shadows they produced. Any other girl would use it as an excuse to hold onto a guy – but not Angela.

She could be anywhere; the orchid was huge and really dark. How would I ever find her? I quickly discarded the idea to call out to her; my voice already sounded way to loud when I was talking normal, screaming was out.

My eyes narrowed as I scanned the darkness all around me. Nothing moved, not even a little hint to tell me which way to go. I could feel my pulse starting to quicken. Hopefully she hadn't gone far enough to get lost .Was that even possible?

I shrugged in response to my own silent worry. There was no reason to get too freaked out; she was probably watching me. I turned in a slow circle, just when I was about to give up and start worrying full out, she was suddenly right in front of my face.

"Boo," she called softly, breaking into quiet laughter. "You should have seen your face."

"That wasn't funny," I sulked. Where did she even come from?

Chapter Six

"It was a little funny," she argued with a small, self-satisfied smile.

"You had me worried." I thrust my chin in her general direction, still irritated, but glad she was alright and not hiding anymore.

"It's nice that you were worried about me." Her lips turned up into a ghost of a smile.

Of course she would take it the wrong way. "You ready to leave now?"

She shrugged and her hint of a smile disappeared again, leaving her looking washed out and sad. My eyes narrowed, causing my eyebrows to dip low on my forehead. Had something happened at her house? Is that why she came looking for me tonight?

Would it really hurt anything for me to be nice to Angela? Before I could make up my mind, she held her hand out between us, palm side up.

"You want to hold hands?" I teased.

"I want to show you something," she replied, not pretending to be embarrassed like other girls would.

"What is it?"

She shook her head until her messy ball of hair wobbled. "I have to show you," she insisted.

"Just tell me one thing," I held a finger in the air, "does it bite?"

Her eyes lit up with her wide smile. "Of course not."

"Good enough," I sighed, putting my hand in hers.

It was strange following Angela through the orchid in the middle of the night. It was certainly at the top of my list of things I never expected to do in my life. More than once, I tried to pull her off her mission and back to the truck.

She refused to be distracted, though.

"Where are we going," I asked, lowering my voice to a whisper.

"Nowhere scary," she laughed back.

"I'm not scared," I lied. Truthfully, I was more than a little freaked out. And only a little bit of that had to do with stealing my brothers truck and driving across town without a license. "I just think we should leave soon."

"So you keep saying," she grinned back at me, her full lips puckering out when she tried to pull a straight face. "Look," she dropped my hand to point to a large cement structure.

I stared at it, trying to make sense of the wildly glowing weeds and cracked cement. It was a fountain – at least what was left of a fountain. Obviously, the structure hadn't felt water in many, many years.

"Isn't it beautiful?" Angela gushed, her face bursting into a wide smile that almost made the night a little bit brighter.

"Yeah," I whispered before I could stop myself. I cleared my throat loudly. "I mean no, it's just a crappy old fountain. Probably falls apart at the lightest touch."

"It will not," she sulked.

"It might."

"Let's see then, shall we?" With that, she bounced forward and propelled herself up on top of the crumbling fountain. "So far, so good," she grinned back at me.

"Come down from there," I warned, eyeing the beaten looking fountain with trepidation. It looked like it was about to crumble under her weight. True – she wouldn't fall very far, but still.

"It's sturdy," she giggled, barely sparing me a glance as she continued her solitary trek around the rim of the old fountain.

"It doesn't look too sturdy."

"You worry too much."

I laughed, the sound booming around the space of the fountain. "I think I have good reason tonight."

"Maybe so," she agreed, only half serious.

"Just get down. That's all I need – for you to fall and we have to go to the emergency room."

"If I do fall, I won't get hurt." Even though she rolled her eyes, she stopped walking and plopped down to sit on the fountain. "Feel better?" She asked, raising one bushy eyebrow high on her forehead.

"Not really." I shoved my hands in my pants pocket, looking around us at the odd shapes the dead trees made. There were no trees by the fountain, but their absence certainly didn't make me feel any better.

"Jacob," she called softly, letting my name fall off her lips and linger in the air between us.

"What?" I called back, shoving my hands deeper into my pockets.

"Come here and sit beside me." She patted the cracked space beside her, smiling as if she'd just invited me to sit on her couch at home.

Not that I'd ever been on her couch at home. Of course not. Was that what she would be expecting after tonight – for me to hang out at her house with her?

"I'm not going to," I answered both her and the internal battle she didn't know about.

"You're just going to stand there all night?" She teased, catching the tip of her tongue between her front teeth.

"Not all night," I teased back, despite my resolve not to be her friend. "We're not going to be staying here that long."

"We're already here," she rolled her eyes. "We might as well enjoy it while we're here."

"And what," I chuckled, "sitting on that crummy fountain is supposed to be fun?"

"Maybe," she laughed. "Come on and sit down."

"I…" I let my tongue glide slowly across my top lip, vaguely aware that I was caving in to her.

Crazy Angela; and I was just going to chill next to her on an ancient fountain in the decaying orchid in the middle of the night.

I was losing my mind.

"Alright," I sighed, "we can sit here for a little while."

Her grin widened.

Chapter Seven

“I'm glad you brought me out here, Jacob," she said in a low voice.

"No problem," I lied with a tight smile that grew despite myself. "It's actually not that bad, being out here with you."

It was the truth, I realized with a start. I would have rather I been day light and I would have rather not have had to break the law to get here, but it wasn't so bad hanging out with Angela.

"You're not so bad either." She smiled, but it wasn't the same smile that she usually wore. It didn't claw at my heart and make it race until I could barely breath.

It was sad.

"What's with the face?"

"What do you mean?" She pushed against her chin and left cheek. "It's the one I was born with."

"You look like you just lost your best friend."

"I don't have a best friend," she shrugged. "You're the only friend I have."

"That's not true." Even I wasn't quite sure which part of her statement I was denying. She saved me the awkward task of explaining by assuming she already knew.

"But it is true, I don't have any other friends," she looked over at me. "Only you."

"Only me?" I grinned. "Sounds like a bad country song to me."

"Maybe," she conceded thoughtfully.

And more to give myself something else to look at and not stare at her for too long, I tilted my head to scan the sky for stars. It was all dark. It wasn't that surprising, really. I figured a storm was rolling in.

"No stars up there," I pointed jerkily skyward. "It's all dark."

"The stars are dying," she muttered.

"It's cloudy." I corrected.

"I remember when I was little and couldn't find the stars," she reminisced fondly, "I thought they were dying." She looked over at me, her violet eyes piercing into my soul. "You don't think stars can die?"

"No," I mumbled, not blinking.

"Everything dies, Jacob."

"It's just cloudy," I insisted, refusing to let her weird mood make me weird too.

"Still." She sighed heavily

We fell into silence, a silence I wasn't sure how to break. I didn't have to worry about it though, Angela was the one to speak first.

"Life isn't fair sometimes," she said slowly, in a lower voice than I was used to hearing from her.

"Did you expect it to be?" I asked, crinkling my nose slightly.

"No," she replied sadly, "I guess not."

"Where is this coming from?" I nudged her ribs lightly with my elbow. "I thought we were supposed to be having fun."

"It's my dad."

"Where?" I sat up quickly, too quickly, and scanned the darkness with wild eyes.

"Not here," she clarified.

"Then…" I grumbled, annoyed at my own paranoia.

"He's all alone."

"Alone?" She said the weirdest things sometimes.

"All alone."

"He's probably sleeping." Logically he would be sleeping, considering it was the middle of the night.

"He might be sleeping," she nodded, a small, sad smile punching me directly in the chest.

"Yeah," I patted her arm lightly, pulling my fingers quickly away. "So you don't have to worry about him."

"I don't mean tonight."

I pressed my lips together, not sure what to say; not really quite sure what she meant.

"I mean…in life."

"Uhh…" Why was she worried about that?

"It's sad really," she continued in her morose voice, "how he hides."

Still confused, I kept my silence this time.

"Sad people always hide from the rest of the world."

"Why is he sad? Did something happen?"

"I guess he's been sad since he lost my mom."

I shifted uncomfortably on the cool fountain. She was talking about her mom again? "It makes sense though."

"What does?" She asked sharply.

"That he would be sad," I shrugged.

"He shouldn't hide though."

I was shocked, deep down shocked, to see her eyes fill with moisture. No matter what she was asking me to do, I was going to agree. Anything to stop her tears.

"We'll help him," I hurried to promise. "I'll help him."

"You will?" She asked in a thick voice.

"Yeah, of course."

"How?"

"We'll make sure he doesn't hide anymore. Get him out there, find him a hobby. I don't know, something."

Even as I watched her wipe away the few tears that had leaked out of her amazing violet eyes, I had to wonder if we would be able to help her dad. Maybe he didn't want our help.

How would two kids like me and Angela know how adults worked? Maybe you only got one chance at love. If that was true, then my mom was in the same boat as Angela's dad. They had both lost their loves.

"Did adults get over stuff like that? But still, was it our job to try and fix them if they didn't?

Somehow, I didn't think so. It was like Angela said – life wasn't always fair. But it was like that for everyone; not just our parents.

All any of us could do was take it one day at a time and do our best with what we had.

"You're a really good guy, Jacob," Angela said, looking over at me.

Chapter Eight

A lot of things went through my head as I sat there on that old fountain staring at Angela. The way her eyes shone extra bright with the tears she hadn't shed, the deep lines running across her bottom lip – as if she had spent a lot of time chewing on the skin there, and the fact that she was leaning towards me.

I wondered what it would look like if I freed her long hair from the hair tie she almost always wore. How far down her back would it go? Would it be curly or just really messy? I couldn't imagine that I'd be able to run my hands through it like couples did in the movies; still I wanted to see it hanging down.

My eyes travelled back down her face to rest on her lips. Her bottom lip jutted out further than anyone else's I knew.

Was it as soft as it looked? What would it feel like pressed against my own lips?

If I just leaned in a little bit, I would be in the perfect position to find out. My whole body seemed to tighten up though, not allowing me to move those few inches.

"You know," she said, suddenly turning away from me, "I've never kissed anyone before."

"Oh." I turned my head so I could look straight out too. How did she know I had just been thinking about kissing her?

"Kissed a boy, I mean," she unnecessarily clarified.

"I know what you meant," I said quickly, giving away my own nervousness.

"I've never even wanted to kiss a boy before."

"And now?" I blurted out the question without thought, then held my breath as I waited for the answer.

"I don't know," she half-whispered.

She didn't know? Did that mean she had been thinking about kissing me too? Did girls even think of things like that? Or was it only guys?

The truth was, I had never kissed anyone either, I had come close last summer with Shelly, but lost my nerve somewhere in the middle. That had been embarrassing – a lot more awkward than being here with Angela.

Still – I couldn't just blurt out that I was a 15, almost 16 year old guy, and I had never even kissed a girl before.

"I...uh..." I looked down at my hands to avoid her penetrating gaze.

"You what?" She prompted, nudging my toe with her own. "You feel sorry for me?"

"No," I scowled.

"You've kissed...ten girls?"

"Of course not," I chuckled lightly, alarmed at the chocked sound. "Quit guessing."

"Then what?" She laughed. Out of the corner of my eye, I saw her shift back.

"I've never kissed anyone either," I admitted in a rush.

"What?" She asked loudly, her lips curling up into a disbelieving smile.

"Yeah," I shrugged, hoping I was coming off as cool instead of lame.

"I don't believe you," she declared.

"Well, it's true." My face still felt too warm, considering the chill in the air.

"You've had girlfriends," she pointed out.

"So?"

"You didn't kiss?"

"Nope."

"What did you do?"

"I don't know...talk?"

One of her eyebrows shot high on her forehead.

"Play video games," I quickly amended.

"I still don't know if I believe you."

"Las summer," I began, my face growing uncomfortably hot, "I almost kissed someone."

"Shelly Benson?"

I nodded, my mouth going way too dry.

"What do you mean almost?" Her nose scrunched up. "How do you almost kiss?"

"Well, it..." I ran my tongue across my bottom lip. Was it possible that I was trying to tell Angela about the most awkward moment I'd ever had?

"Did her breath stink?"

"No. Her brother was there and..."

"Why was her brother there?" Angela cut across my mumbling.

"He drove us to the movies." I puffed out my cheeks, determined not to say anymore about it.

"So you chickened out," she said more than asked, nodding her head as if she knew all about awkward almost kisses that were embarrassing to think about.

"I didn't chicken out," I scowled. "It just wasn't the right time."

"Do you think now is the right time?" She asked in a rush of low words.

"Now?" I glanced around us – not exactly romantic.

"Yeah," her voice gained strength. "Will you kiss me, Jacob?"

"Um..." I looked over at her, just to be sure she was serious. She was.

"Don't you want to?" She asked, her eyes widening slightly.

"I do." I swallowed loudly.

Whoever heard of a planned kiss? Weren't these things supposed to just happen naturally?

True, I had been thinking of what it would be like to kiss her, but actually doing it was different. Part of me just wanted to get up and bolt. The saner part of me refused to move.

"Ok," she nodded a little, staring up at me with those blue-purple eyes of hers.

"Ok," I whispered back, leaning forward just enough that there was barely any space between our faces.

Then suddenly, one of us moved, I wasn't even sure which one, and our lips met.

Chapter Nine

She kept her eyes closed even after I had pulled away from her. I watched her face, wondering why she was looking like that.

Did I do something wrong? Maybe I shouldn't have kissed her. She probably thought I was some kind of perv now; bringing her out here just to grope her.

But no, I told myself, she had wanted to kiss me too. And really, it was her idea to come to the orchid. What did she think happened out here?

Finally, her eyes fluttered back open. "Well," she said slowly, "it wasn't really that good – was it?"

I let out a bark of a laugh, the kind that just explodes from your chest after you spend so much time being tense. "It wasn't?" I laughed again.

"Not like I thought it would be," she said thoughtfully, screwing her forehead up until it was all lined.

"It wasn't that bad," I contradicted.

"I guess," she conceded slowly.

Laughing even more, I wrapped my arms around her shoulders and pulled her body close to mine until her head was resting against my shoulder. "You're so weird," I whispered into her hair after several warm moments.

She pulled gently away from me, keeping her hands resting against my arm. I suddenly wished I wasn't wearing a jacket so I could feel her fingers brushing against my skin.

"I'm glad we came out here," I gushed out, my voice barely above a whisper.

"Are you?" She returned my smile.

Maybe I would get the chance to improve that first kiss. My dad always said if you wanted to be good at something, you needed to practice. I had just decided to lean forward when she spoke again.

"I'm ready to go now," she abruptly announced.

"Uhh..you are?"

"I thought you said you were ready to go?" She reminded me, getting back up on two legs.

"We...we don't have to," I stammered. "It's like you said, we're already out here."

She tilted her head to look up at the sky, revealing her long, white neck. "I think we've probably been out here long enough."

I looked up too, wondering if she could somehow know the time from looking at the stars. I knew some people could tell by looking at the sun, maybe it worked the same way with stars. There were none up there though.

"Alright," I reluctantly agreed, standing up next to her.

The trees that had obligingly fallen into the background while we had been sitting, now sprang back up with existence. Looking through them to the paths they hid, I felt a thrill of trepidation.

We hadn't exactly been paying too much attention to direction as we ran through them before, playing a twisted game of hide and seek. I wasn't all that sure we would be able to find our way back to the truck.

"Do you know which way?" I asked nervously.

"Of course," she shrugged, as if finding our way through a bunch of trees was an every day thing.

Maybe it was for her. There was a lot I didn't know about Angela Lake. We had lived next to each other for years, but I hadn't taken the time to know her in quite awhile.

As soon as I realized the other kids didn't like her, actually. Guilt and a brand new sense of regret made me look away from her.

She caught my hand, reclaiming my attention. "it's not far," she promised.

Warmth spread through my fingers and travelled quickly throughout my body. I smiled, easily letting her lead the way.

"Hey look," she pointed up at the night sky. "The stars are back again."

I followed her out stretched hand. Sure enough, little white bursts of light now dotted the blackness. "I figured it would rain," I commented, holding my hand that wasn't attached to hers palm side up.

"They say in the movies that we aren't supposed to talk about the weather," she giggled, tucking her chin into her arm.

"They weren't talking about us," I teased, "they were talking about boring people."

"Oh," she sing-songed the single syllable. "We're definitely not boring," she agreed.

"Of course not," I tried to say with a straight face, but failed.

"You're really cool, Jacob," she announced without any of the awkwardness someone else saying those words would have had.

"Thanks...I guess." I couldn't pull off the same smoothness.

"And brave."

"Yeah?"

"If your dad was still alive, he would've been so proud of the man you're becoming."

My smile slipped.

"Jacob," she turned slightly to smile up at me, "I think you're going to be amazing."

My heart lurched at her words and although it fell back to it's proper place in my chest, it still hammered away much faster than usual.

The trees suddenly didn't look so creepy either, as if the moonlight that continued to play peek-a-boo in the cloudy night sky was giving them life.

Or maybe it was just the girl walking next to me.

It was how she made me feel that made all the difference. It was a strange feeling, one I wasn't sure if I was completely comfortable with. I would worry about that later though, now just wasn't the time.

We reached the truck just a few minutes after we left the fountain. It seemed much further in, but as Angela promised, it wasn't that far.

I waited until Angela situated herself on the passenger side so I could close the door for her. Then I rounded the front of the truck and slid into the drivers seat.

"Ready?" I asked, wiggling my eyebrows in her direction.

"Yep." She grinned, sucking in a quick breath and holding it there.

Chapter Ten

The truck roared to life, making both of us jump inside the cab. "Whoa," I breathed out.

"Was it that loud before?" Angela wondered out loud. "Do you think an animal crawled up into the engine?"

"No." I sat back against the seat. Could that happen? "It would have ran out, right?"

"I don't know," she shrugged.

We both pressed our faces against the door windows, searching the ground for any scuttling creatures. There was nothing out there as far as I could see.

"It's fine," I told us both. "It's just loud because it's so quiet out here."

She nodded, but continued to search outside for any small creatures.

Not altogether reassured, I backed my brother's truck back out onto the road that would take us home. Angela sat back in the seat, folding her hands comfortably across her lap.

Although she wasn't crying anymore, I still saw the sadness in the way she held her mouth and in the crinkle of her deep eyes.

Was she still thinking about her dad? I turned my attention back to the road in front of me.

The road stretched out ahead of the truck like a dark river. It seemed so ordinary after spending so long amidst the dead, dancing trees.

I peeked across the seat at Angela. She was sitting very still, staring out at the road. Was she seeing it the same way I was – that it was entirely too normal?

No, I decided with a small frown. Angela would never look at things the same way I did. But maybe that was ok.

What would happen now? Tomorrow when I woke up again?

I didn't want to go back to ignoring her and trying to pretend I didn't notice her. We lived right next to each other so it wouldn't be hard to talk and get to know each other properly.

No one would actually have to know, it wasn't like we were going to start making out in the halls at school or anything. Our lockers weren't next to each other and we didn't sit beside each other in any classes.

My heart sank a little at the thought of how little we saw each other at school.

It wasn't enough just to talk to her in secret though, I realized. I wanted to be Angela's friend – all the time. Maybe even more than that.

What would everyone say if me and Angela started going out? I tried to imagine telling people she was my girlfriend. Uncomfortable images flashed through my mind.

My friends, who often made fun of the strange girl who wore baggy shirts and didn't brush her hair, would think I had lost my mind. They might not even talk to me anymore.

And Shelly Benson.

My lips snarled up at the thought of Shelly and her friends. The breakup hadn't been exactly a mutual decision. I knew, just like everyone else knew, that Shelly wanted to get back together with me.

Before tonight, I had been considering it. Not because I liked Shelly much, but because everyone else liked her. If I started going out with Angela instead...

It was weird though. My eyes screwed up into thin slits as my mind whirled with the possibility.

I liked Angela Lake - a lot.

What if I liked her enough to not care what other people said? They didn't know her like I did. They had never been on the receiving end of one of her soul shattering smiles.

Just because the kids we went to school with couldn't see past the hair piled haphazardly on top of her head, or the strange things that came out of her mouth, didn't mean I couldn't.

Angela had told me to be brave. She had even said she thought I was brave. I hadn't ever really given much thought to bravery. It wasn't a word that went with the world today, unless you were a firefighter or soldier or something. It certainly didn't pertain to a 15 year old kid trying to make it through high school.

Then again, maybe it did.

I liked Angela and I wanted to tell her so. I could be brave. Hiding behind fake girlfriends and a false sense of "coolness" didn't make someone happy.

Sad people always hide.

Well, not anymore.

I smiled wide, taking a second to glance over at her again. She was still watching the road as we got close and closer to home.

Just tell her.

I opened my mouth, then pressed my lips tight together again. What was I actually going to say? What would be good enough to make sure she knew how much I liked her and what I was prepared to sacrifice to be next to her?

What would she say if I just said all that? Just put it on the seat between us?

Before I could make up my mind what to say, our houses came into view. I pulled into the driveway and parked my brothers truck back in the garage. I switched the engine off and leaned back in the seat.

Everything looked the same as when we'd left it. I didn't feel the same, though.

Chapter Eleven

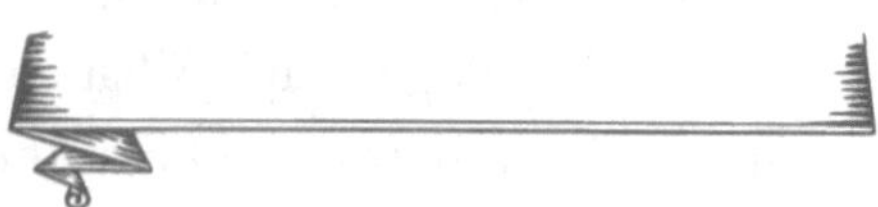

Barely able to reign my wide grin in enough to not look goofy, I glanced over at Angela. She sat quite still on the other side of the truck, in no apparent rush to leave my company.

Surprisingly, or maybe not surprising at all, I didn't mind that she wasn't leaving. An invisible line that I had made myself had been crossed, putting me and Angela on the same side.

And I hadn't felt so light in a really long time.

"So," I began, pushing my hand out in front of me so I could stare at the strange shapes my fingers made in the darkness.

"So," she smiled, nodding her head and still making no move to get out.

"We should do this again sometime," I chuckled. "Maybe after I'm legal though."

She made no response.

Now was the time to tell her how I felt. I puffed out my cheeks, and let the air out in an audible rush. "I like you, Angela," I decided boldly. "I like you a lot, maybe even as more than just friends."

She sucked in a quick breath and let it out again just as fast. Although she wasn't exactly smiling, I could tell she was excited. She probably just didn't know what to say.

For someone like Angela Lake, a simple statement like "I like you" would be hard to get out. If I knew anything about her, she would have to analyze everything I said before she would be able to respond.

Or maybe she didn't like me.

No, I discarded the stray thought. She had called me outside and she had kissed me as much as I had kissed her.

I heard the soft click of her door handle and hurried to follow her out.

"Are you going in?" I asked, hurrying to catch up with her long strides back around to the front of our houses.

"It's late," she responded.

"It's not a school night," I muttered, looking down at my feet.

There on the sidewalk was the butterfly she had drawn before we left. A rush of warmth filled my stomach. "The ninja and the mermaid," I said stupidly.

"It's a butterfly," she corrected.

"The ninja and the mermaid," I pointed to both of us, "found a way to co-exist."

"You should go in," she nodded behind me where my house was still dark.

"I Don't feel tired." I swallowed hard over the lump that made my voice sound warped.

"It has to be really late," she smiled.

"It was really late when you threw rocks at my window," I pointed out, not wanting to leave her company.

"Thank you, Jacob." Her voice caught slightly, making my breath accelerate alongside my heart.

"You're welcome, Angela."

"I'll never forget tonight."

My eyebrows drew together slightly, trying to warn me of something in her voice. "Me either," I vowed.

"Promise?" She asked in a quiet, thick voice.

My smile slipped. "Yeah, I promise."

Her smile beamed bright again at my words. "Goodnight." She rose up on her tiptoes and kissed me softly on the cheek.

"Goodnight," I murmured back. As I walked towards my kitchen door, I glanced back at Angela. She was bent low over her chalk butterfly, not looking at me. My lips curved upwards into a foolish grin.

Once in the kitchen, I slipped the cool metal key back onto the safety of it's peg. I pressed my forehead against the cool, light blue wall, relief making my shoulders sag low.

There was no one in the kitchen waiting for me, so it was a safe bet that Angela would be right – no one would ever know what we had done.

I pushed myself upright and hurried over to the large living room window, hoping to get another glimpse of Angela before she went back inside. By the time I got there, though, she was already gone.

What a strange night it had turned out to be. Running after Angela Lake in the orchid. I shook my head; even if I could tell anyone what I had done – who would believe me?

My thoughts drifted to rest on the sad sort of smile and the strange way she had sounded when she told me goodbye. Something must have happened at her house. Had she fought with her dad? Maybe that was why she was so worried about him.

We all fought with our parents, though .Sometimes adults just didn't understand.

Oh well, I sighed, I would ask her more about it in the morning. We had time. I smiled again and tiptoed up the steps.

Up in my room, my bed was exactly as I had left it just hours before. The thick blue checkered comforter was pulled back to reveal the dark blue sheet mom had gotten me for Christmas last year.

Bypassing the comfort that the bed promised, I went directly to the window. I could still remember the surprise I felt when I looked out this same window and saw Angela Lake standing outside.

I looked up at the sky; no stars were visible.

They had been playing hide and seek the entire night. Just like Angela, I remembered, when she ran through the trees to that old fountain.

The fountain wasn't so bad though, not really. I crawled into bed still grinning as memories replayed in my head. Memories of Angela and the way her lips felt against mine.

Chapter Twelve

When I opened my eyes, the sun was shining brightly through the window. I had left the curtains pulled back the night before so I could watch for the stars to come back. I fell asleep before I saw them again.

The low rumbles coming from my stomach prevented me from staying in bed trying to relive my bizarre night with Angela Lake. I would go see her after breakfast, I decided. Her and her dad since she was so worried about him being alone.

There was a certain spring to my step as I made my way down to the kitchen where my brother Jimmy and his long time girlfriend, Rachel, were already sitting at the round table.

I hesitated, just at the bottom of the steps. Had Jimmy been out to his truck yet? Would he be able to tell that I had driven it?

No way. Not even possible.

"Hey Jake," Rachel called out brightly.

Probably not then.

"You slept late."

"It's not a school day," I shrugged, trying to remember how I had said those exact words to Angela just hours before. "Where's mom?"

"Work," Jimmy answered around a mouthful of food.

I pulled an enormous bowl from the cupboard and filled it with some marshmallow sweetness that I still loved no matter how old I was.

"Wheres the milk?" I asked loudly, scanning the table.

"Fridge," grunted Jimmy, his mouth filled to overflowing.

Grumbling slightly, I got back up and retrieved the partial gallon from the fridge.

"You need a haircut, Jake," rachel complained.

"I barely have any hair," I retorted, running my hand over the short strands.

"Whatever," she rolled her eyes.

"I thought mom didn't have to work this weekend," I commented, pouring milk over my cereal.

"There was an accident sometime last night," Rachel answered, "so she got called in to help."

"Really?" I asked with my own mouth full. "Was it bad?"

"A girl died."

"What?"

"She was your age, you might know her."

"Who is it?" I asked, swallowing the cereal down in a thick clump.

"You know her," Jimmy piped in, "she lived next door."

My heart skidded to a stop then raced back to working again.

"Angela Lake lived next door to you?" Rachel asked, crinkling her nose. "It's really sad – what happened to her."

"What are you saying," I asked loudly, pulling the cereal box she was reaching for out of her hands. "Don't joke around about this."

"I'm not," she snarled, her eyes widening with irritation. "Angela and her dad got in a bad accident last night. She died before the ambulance even got there."

"No," I blurted out, shaking my head. "What time?"

"How should I know? I wasn't there."

"What time?" I repeated, barely able to hear anything over the roar of my own heart. She was with me at 1:30 AM so I knew she was wrong.

"Probably like 1:30," she shrugged. "That's when Matt got the call."

"That's...that's not even...possible." My chair scraped loudly across the linoleum as I hastily stood up and flung the door open.

She's not dead. She can't be dead. No. It's not possible.

I didn't acknowledge Jimmy and Rachel's question as I hurried around to the front of the house. Dropping to my knees on the ground, I could just make out the faint chalk drawing of a butterfly. The initials JW and Al were no longer visible.

I looked up at the house next door All was quiet and dark. "Angela," I whispered.

I leaned low over the counter where a woman with short red hair sat typing very quickly. She looked up, a fake smile plastered all over her face.

"Yes dear?" She asked thickly.

"Which room is Mr. Lake in?" I asked quietly, half wishing she would tell me he wasn't there.

"The man from the car accident?" She asked, her smile slipping.

"Yeah." My heart sank.

"401. Are you family?"

"Yeah."

"I'm so sorry, dear," she said sadly. "That poor girl, and only 15 years old."

I turned away before she could say anything else, she had already said too much.

I made my way through the single story hospital until I came to a door marked 401. My finger traced the small number several times before I realized what I was doing. I shoved my hands in my pocket.

Laying in the hospital bed, just recognizable through the tubes and bandages, was Angela's father. Something sharp stung my eyes.

Somehow, without any word from me, my legs carried me forward until I was right next to Mr. Lake's bed. An uninviting brown chair was pulled close to the side. Once again, my body worked on it's own and I found myself sitting down – staring at the broken man in the hospital bed.

Scattered memories fought for control in my numb brain, images of the night before. Angela sitting on that old fountain, Angela in the seat next to me in my brother's truck, Angela's lips pressed against mine.

This wasn't possible.

"Hi Mr. Lake," I greeted thickly in a voice I barely recognized. "I'm Jake Winston," Angela..." My voice broke slightly, "she was my friend."

He didn't say anything, he just stared at me with eyes the same blue-violet as hers. Neither of us said anything.

"Life isn't fair sometimes. Sad people hide away from the world and stay all alone."

"Maybe we're all sad."

"Maybe we shouldn't hide anymore."

Maybe not, I sighed, sitting back further into the chair.

THANK YOU FOR READING!!

Sneak Peek of "THE DEATH OF ME"

Chapter One

My lungs filled up with air so suddenly that it made me gasp. Coughing and sputtering, I pressed my hand to my heaving chest. I was pretty sure my eyes were open but everything around me was dark so I couldn't be absolutely sure.

Where am I?

It was hard to remember much of anything, even my name felt just out of reach, so there was no way I could recall where I was. Or, even more puzzling, why I was lying down. This wasn't my bed, right? My forehead creased with the swirling thoughts.

I groaned loudly and tried to pull my legs up. They wouldn't move. No need to panic, I told my heart when it tried to speed up. Everything was fine.

"Wh..." I felt around me, my fingers sliding over rough pavement. *Am I outside?*

I turned my head to one side, hoping to figure out which street I was laying in. Please don't be somewhere public. How embarrassing would it be if I passed out in front of everyone at Jimmy Vale's end of summer party.

Oh yeah.

Tyler had taken me to Jimmy's party. I bought a new dress just for the occasion. Everyone who was anyone went to that party – of course I went. But there was drinking. I must have had too much.

"Ugh." My head hurt. *You can't just lay here all night.*

Groaning some more, I pushed my hands out in front of me. I seemed to be wrapped in some sort of blanket. Clearly some drunk idiot thought it would be funny to wrap a drunk girl up like a taco. If Tyler had anything to do with this, I thought savagely, he will pay.

Fighting my way out of the blanket, I used the wall next to me to pull myself slowly to my feet. My legs were shaking so bad, I wasn't entirely sure they would hold me up. Only after I was up did I realize that it wasn't night after all – it was day time.

Although I wasn't sure how it was possible, I was in some sort of alley. From the looks of things, it appeared that I had slept behind a dumpster. My teeth clenched together. I was seriously going to kill Tyler.

I glanced down at the ground, my eyes falling on my ruined dress on the way. "What the hell?" My new dress was torn around the bottom and one strap was hanging off my shoulder. This dress cost a fortune. Dad was going to kill me. "Shit."

My shoes were gone too. Had someone seriously stolen my shoes? They were my favorite pair. Hopefully, I had left them at the party and I'd be able to get them back.

I shook my head quickly from side to side. This didn't make any sense. Even if I did leave the party, why on earth would I come to sleep in this disgusting place? Even if I was drunk – really drunk.

I would have gone home.

All along my arms were long scratch marks of blood, frayed skin, and dirt. They didn't hurt though – thank goodness. I pressed one finger to a spot, testing it, and there was no pain. I mean, they looked hideous of course, but it was a relief that I didn't have to add pain to my list of grievances.

What's the last thing you remember?

Tyler and I had gotten in a huge fight in front of everyone, I recalled.

Why?

He was kissing that slut – Cassie Andrews.

"Oh crap," I pressed a hand to my throbbing forehead. I had said a lot of things; most of them to Cassie. Still, that didn't explain how I had ended up in the alley.

I hobbled out from behind the dumpster that was hiding me. At the far end of the short alley I could see the street. I didn't recognize it but there would be people there. *I can't let anyone see me like this.*

The torn dress didn't have pockets so I had left my cell in Tyler's car when we got to the party. It looked like whoever had left me didn't even bother making sure I had a phone.

My scowl deepened.

A spider scuttled to the top of the wall I was leaning on. Whimpering loudly, I yanked my hand back to the safety of my own body. Oh my word, what kind of maniac left someone to sleep here?

The ground under me was littered with empty bottles and plastic bags filled with things I didn't want to think about. "Gross." Scrunching my nose, I stepped over a pile of trash, only to land my bare feet in something wet. Things kept getting worse.

I couldn't just curl back up and go to sleep though; I needed to make my way out of the alley and find a way to get back home. I had no choice. I took another step, then another.

Once I was out of the shadows that had taken over the alley, the sun blared down on me. It seemed out of place – to be so sunny and cheerful when I looked like I had just been in a car accident.

Sniffing back my indignation, I scanned the sidewalk for someone who looked approachable. There weren't that many people and most of them had their jackets wrapped tightly to their bodies, as if they had just robbed a bank and were hiding the evidence. Which, by the looks of this place, might not be far off.

A woman stopped nearby and brought her phone to her ear. "Hello?" she barked into the small device. "No. I can't do that." Her lips pressed together angrily, making me hesitate on approaching her. "It's your turn to pick the kid up," she practically screamed. I could actually see the spit flying from her mouth. *Ew.*

"Excuse me," I squeaked. I was just desperate enough to ask a complete stranger to let me use their spit covered phone. I had seriously hit rock bottom. The woman didn't even glance my way before hurrying off.

Imagine me, Avery Lewis, getting ignored by some *homeless* lady in the slums. I pressed my lips tighter together. Had I fallen into the twilight zone or something?

Searching for another person with a phone, my eyes fell on a single blue door in an otherwise plain brick wall. It was strangely out of place, why was there a door there?

Public Bath, the small sign above the door read. Hopefully they just couldn't afford the rest of the letters because I couldn't imagine anyone taking a bath in public.

I must have been filthy, I decided. That's why the woman didn't let me use her phone. Maybe she thought I was asking for money. Horrified, I hurried inside what I hoped was a bathroom.

The only mirror above the long row of sinks was dirty – it matched the rest of the bathroom perfectly – but it was clean enough for me to see my reflection. My mouth fell open in horror at the sight.

"Oh my word." I forced my jaw to close. Who knew what I was breathing in?

I had seen my hair every day for the past seventeen years; it had never, ever been so dirty. I couldn't even see the honey colored curls with blonde highlights that mom paid for every month, now it was just one blob of brown filth.

Using the one paper towel that was still on the roll, I scrubbed off some of the dirt streaks on my face. I wouldn't be able to get clean in here though, I needed to get home and take a real shower. Maybe three showers. Even my fingernails were thick with dirt. What the hell happened to me?

"Damn brats," a harsh voice crackled from the doorway. A woman with wild looking hair bustled inside, her lips pulled down into a pointed frown. "What the hell are you looking at?" she barked at me.

"Nothing," I squeaked, then hurried back outside. Even if that woman had a phone, no way would she let me use it. No way would I want to; I'd probably get lice. A shudder ran up my spine.

The street had gotten busier in the short time I was in that disgusting bathroom. People rushed past me, not even glancing up as they went by. If it wasn't strictly against my own personal rules, I would have given in to the tears that were beginning to sting the corners of my eyes.

I just need to call home; Mom will come pick me up. I was willing to risk her horror just to get out of here.

But how could I do that if no one stopped to let me use their phone?

"Hey," I called out to a guy that couldn't be much older than me. All the boys in school wanted to date me so there was no reason this one wouldn't stop and try to help. Damsel in distress and all that bullshit.

He hesitated on the corner of the street, looking all around him. "Hey," I screamed louder. "I need your help." He pulled his jacket closer to his body and hurried on, not looking behind him where I was standing.

"It's not even cold," I wailed after him. "All I have on is this torn dress. Are you even human?"

It wasn't just the guy that ignored me though, no one on the crowded street looked my way. Even if they didn't want to help; a young, beautiful girl was standing alone in a tattered dress. Why weren't they staring?

Angry, cold, embarrassed, and getting scared – I spotted a young woman hurrying up the street and decided to take action. "I need your phone," I blurted out, stepping in front of her. "I just need to call my mom, I promise I'll give it right back. I can even pay you." I didn't have any money on me, but I was sure I had more money in my piggy bank than she made in a month.

She walked right through me; all I saw was black.

VERY SUDDENLY, I WAS laying down again. But not in the alley this time.

I sat up slowly, confused. Somehow – even though it was impossible – I was in my own back yard. The grass was cold on my legs, tiny drops of dew made my dress damp.

Dad usually kept the lawn trimmed and perfect but he was working on some big case and had been neglecting it. I had listened to many arguments over the breakfast table about hiring someone to do it; dad refused. Apparently, this grass was the only thing that gave him purpose.

How did I get here though? Was that alley and the street just a dream? That woman had just walked right through me, as if…

But no, it had to have been a dream.

I held my hands out in front of me, they shook like crazy. And they were caked in dirt. Scratches of dirt and blood streaked all the way up my arms, my dress was torn and splattered with blood, my shoes were gone. So it wasn't *all* a dream.

I took a deep breath and let it out again through my nose, closing my eyes in the process. "Don't lose control, Avery," I whispered in a shaking breath. Was all of me shaking?

What did I have to be afraid of now? I swallowed hard past the bile of nerves that had risen in the back of my throat. No matter how it had happened, at least I was home again. I was safe here; this was the place I had been trying to get to.

I couldn't let mom and dad see me like this though, they would never let me leave the house again. I had begged to be allowed to go to that party – I needed a shower.

Mom had always made sure that the side door that led to the garage be left unlocked during the day "in case one of us came home early and forgot their key". For once, I was grateful for what I usually considered a lack of good sense.

Opening the door just enough to squeeze myself inside, I leaned back against the inside of the door. I had never realized before how clean our garage was. Only my own small blue car was in it this morning. Mom and dad would be at work; who knew where Lindsey was. I didn't really care either, it was better that she was gone. I would never hear the end of it if she saw me like this.

The fear of getting caught spurred me forward again.

I quickly punched in the code to unlock the kitchen door and slipped inside. I didn't really expect anyone to be there but I couldn't deny my relief to find it empty. On the white board that was stuck to the fridge was a message from my sister, Lindsey. "Went for lunch with Lucy. XO Linds." Mom insisted on notes whenever we left the house, she liked to know where we were.

My breath, that I didn't realize I had been holding, whooshed out of my lungs. "Thank god," I told the immaculate kitchen counter, "at least I don't have to worry about that beast seeing me."

Still, I didn't want to stay in the kitchen too long. Being around so much white made me feel even dirtier – if that was possible. I tip toed quickly up the wide staircase and into the second bedroom on the right.

My room.

Oh, so much better.

I wanted nothing more than to fall face first onto my bed and sleep for at least a week. But that wasn't possible. I was way too dirty; the bed spread that was tucked perfectly around the soft mattress was too clean. The pink flowers that swirled on the pillowcase were dainty and perfect, that was no place to lay this head. First, a shower.

There was no point in being careful with my clothes now that the dress was ruined. I pulled at the remaining intact strap and yanked hard enough for it to rip. The fabric slid down my body into a tattered heap at my feet. I kicked it into the corner with the intention to get rid of it later; mom didn't come in my bathroom often enough for me to worry much about it now though.

Flipping on the water in the bathtub, I inhaled deeply. Steam billowed out all around my face until I could almost feel the dirt falling off of my skin. Now that there was more light, I turned back to the mirror.

"Oh my word." I didn't even look like myself. There were dirt rings around my neck and wrists, even my toes were dirty. That wasn't surprising since I didn't have shoes on. Who knew how long I had been running around in my bare feet? Unable to look anymore, I stepped into the shower.

As soon as the water hit my body, a trail of dirt started on the bottom of the pristine white tub. It took two rounds of shampoo for my hair to feel clean enough; the water ran cold before I got out from under the streaming water.

Wrapping a large towel around my now clean body, I made my way back out into my room. I didn't really care what I wore, as long as it was clean and all in one piece. A pair of light grey sweats that flared out by my feet and a pink tee shirt that clung to my chest were the first things I grabbed.

It wasn't my best but still cute, I decided with a small huff.

The scratches on my arms were still visible but looked much better. In fact, upon closer inspection, they may have been caused by tree branches. Jimmy Vale had woods all around his place. It was possible...

With a small sigh I sank on to my vanity chair. Mom had bought me the ornate vanity set when I was just eight years old. *You're never too young to look your best*, she had trilled as she organized the brush set for me.

And I really did look so much better without the mud caked to my face and my hair. Light blue eyes stared at me from the oval mirror, they were unsure about what had happened last night but grateful that no one had seen me in that state.

Stuck in the corner of the oval mirror was a picture of the Triple Threat - me, Nina and Billie. The three of us had bonded with each other in the third grade and decided to take over the school together. Nina was exotic with her brown hair and brown eyes. Billie was our red-haired beauty; she knew exactly how to get the boys on our side.

And then there was me.

Just where were my friends last night? We had promised to stay together and keep ourselves out of trouble. Then I woke up in an alley rolled up in an old sleeping bag. So much for that promise.

"Oh well," I shook my head lightly. I was home now. I would talk to the girls later and find out what had happened, but for now I would just brush my hair.

"One," I pulled my brush through my wet hair.

"Two. "I took a deep breath and glanced again at my reflection. There were still scratches on my neck. Even after the shower I could still see the dirt under my fingernails. Mom would have a fit if she saw me now. She hated dirt. Trying not to think too much about the dirt I continued brushing my hair.

Over and over again.

"Seventy-six." Downstairs, the door opened with a jingle. Dad liked the bell. He said it made him feel safer. It wasn't like a robber would be deterred by a bell though.

Now - the sound was a welcome one. It meant my parents were home; finally something normal. After the morning I had had, normal sounded just fine. I paused with the brush halfway to my head, my ears toward the door. I wasn't disappointed.

"Avery."

I heard my name echo against my door. "I'm up here," I called back.

"Avery, where are you?" Rolling my eyes, I set the brush back on the vanity. Why did Mom have to be so dramatic?

"I'm up here," I screamed louder. "I'm trying to brush my hair." Wasn't she the one that taught me the importance of brushing my hair?

"Lindsey?"

With a loud sigh, I bounced off my seat and hurried out the door. "Mom, you'll never guess where I was this morning." I wouldn't tell her everything, obviously, but I wanted to at least tell her some of it. The shock on her face would be priceless.

I caught sight of mom just as she was going into the kitchen. She didn't look up at me, maybe she didn't hear me.

"Mom!"

"Here's a note from Lindsey," dad told her.

"It looks like she went out to lunch, but why didn't Avery leave a note?"

"I have no idea," dad grumbled in his deep, tired voice. "You know Avery, she was probably just too busy."

"What are you talking about?" I grumbled back, irritated that they were talking about me when I was standing right there.

Mom's lips were pursed. "Where did the girls go last night?" She sniffed.

Dad pulled open the fridge and grabbed out the milk. "Some party," he waved his hand vaguely in the air. "All I know is that Avery had to have a new dress just for it."

"And she never came back home?" Mom's voice was starting to raise.

Oh my word, why were they being so weird? "It's not like I was out all night," I lied. Neither of them turned to look at me. "Hello? Did you hear me?"

"I think I better call Billie or Nina," mom said. "She probably just stayed the night at one of their houses."

"Hey," I shouted. "Mom I'm right here." Starting to panic, I waved my hands frantically in her face. "What's wrong with you Mom? I'm right here."

"I'm sure she'll come home later," dad suggested calmly, flipping open a newspaper. As usual, he refused to get worked up.

"I'm still calling."

"Oh my word," I whispered. "They can't see me." No one in the street could see me either. What was happening to me? Why was I suddenly invisible? How was this even possible? My throat felt closed, I couldn't get a breath in. Just when I wanted to scream- everything went black.

Don't miss out!

Visit the website below and you can sign up to receive emails whenever Amy Richie publishes a new book. There's no charge and no obligation.

https://books2read.com/r/B-A-OGMF-GTTQ

BOOKS 2 READ

Connecting independent readers to independent writers.

Also by Amy Richie

Blood Vine Series
Willow

Clearview Academy
The Death Of A Suspect
The Death of Me

Time To Love
A Second To Breathe
A Minute of Silence
An Hour of Solitude

Standalone
Lark
The Last Tomorrow
Lost and Found

The Seventh Sacrifice
Wren

Watch for more at amyrichie.weebly.com.

About the Author

Amy Richie has lived in a small town her entire life. She lives with her three kids and their cats, George and Ellie. She began writing in high school but never took it seriously until a few years ago. She enjoys writing because it takes her out of her everyday life and gives life to the people in her head. "When I was little I wanted to be a mermaid, then when I was in high school I wanted to be a vampire; now as an adult I'm a writer, which is better because now I get to be both."

Read more at amyrichie.weebly.com.